"I know nothing with any certainty, but
the sight of stars makes me dream."

—Vincent van Gogh

Henry Holt and Company, LLC
Publishers since 1866
175 Fifth Avenue
New York, New York 10010
www.henryholtchildrensbooks.com

Henry Holt® is a registered trademark
of Henry Holt and Company, LLC.
Copyright © 2006 by Denise Fleming
All rights reserved.
Distributed in Canada by H. B. Fenn and Company Ltd.

Library of Congress Cataloging-in-Publication Data
Fleming, Denise.
The cow who clucked / Denise Fleming.—1st ed.
p.   cm.
Summary: When a cow loses her moo, she searches to see if another animal in the barn has it.
ISBN-13: 978-0-8050-7265-5 / ISBN-10: 0-8050-7265-9
[1. Animal sounds—Fiction. 2. Lost and found possessions—Fiction. 3. Cows—Fiction.] I. Title.
PZ7.F5994Cow 2006   [E]—dc22   2005022676

First Edition—2006
Printed in China on acid–free paper. ∞

1   3   5   7   9   10   8   6   4   2

The illustrations were created using colored cotton fiber, hand-cut stencils, and squeeze bottles.
Book design by Denise Fleming and David Powers.

Visit www.denisefleming.com.

The Cow who Clucked

Denise Fleming

Henry Holt and Company • New York

One morning Cow woke up to find
she had lost her moo.

"The first thing I must do," said Cow,

"is find my moo!"

And off she went.

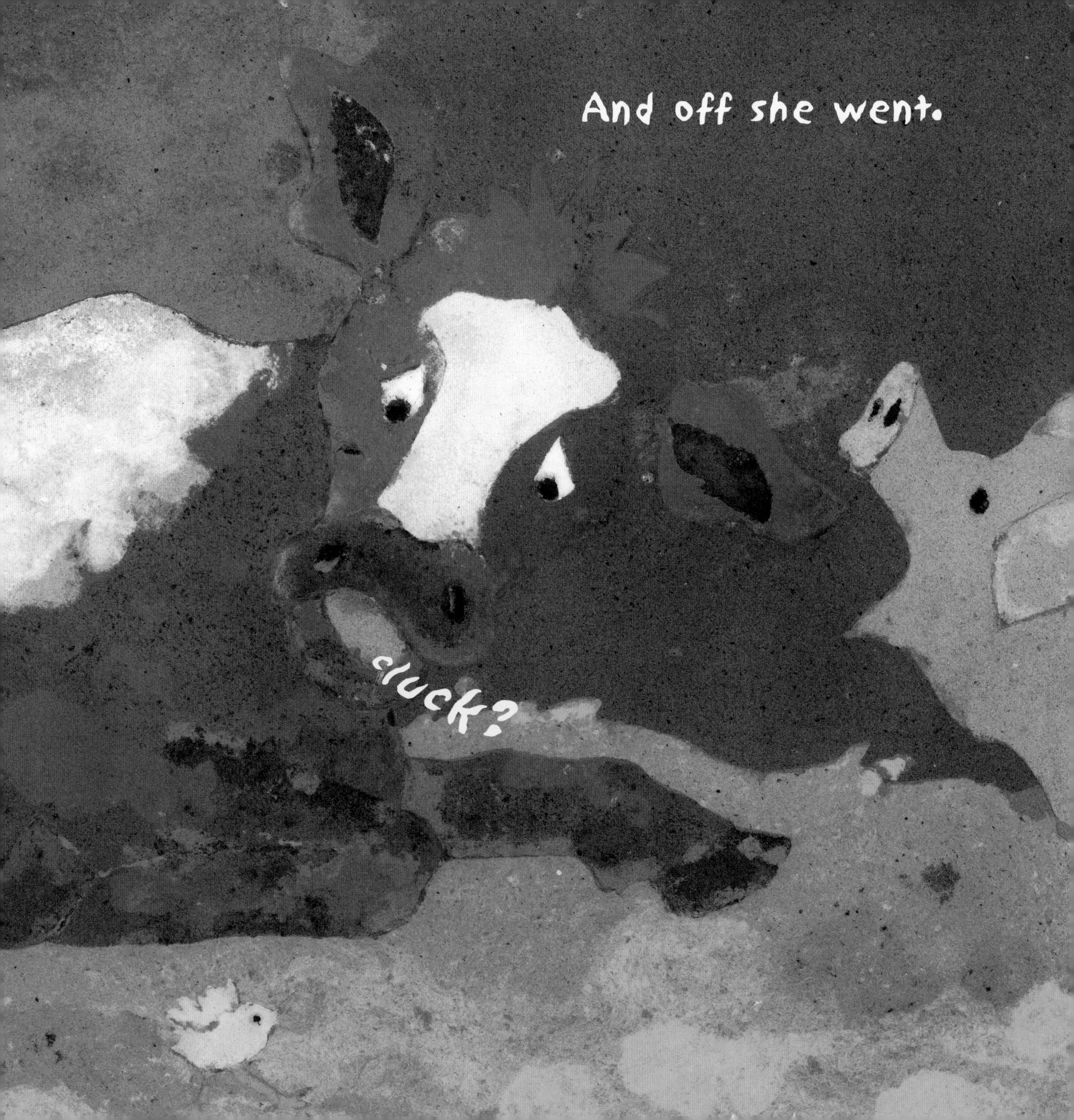

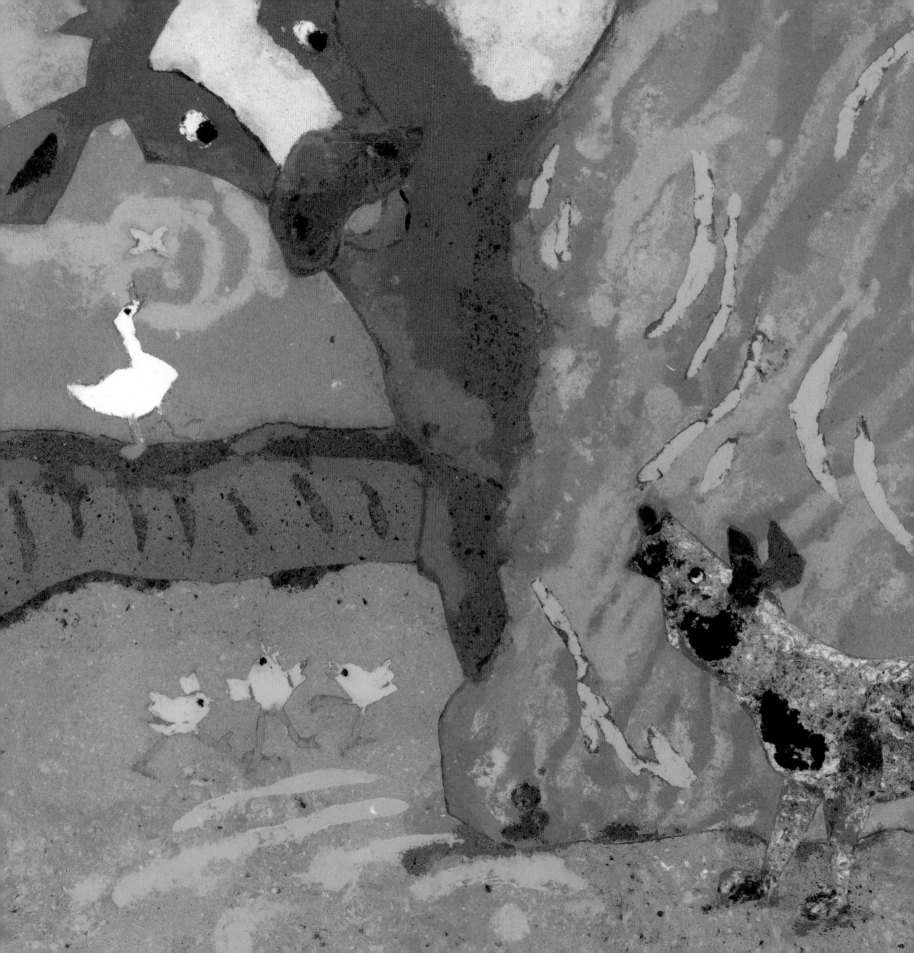

Cow met Dog.

"**Cluck, cluck,**" said Cow.

"**Warf, warf,**" said Dog.

"It is not you who has my moo," said Cow.

And on she went.

Cow stopped to nibble grass.
"Cluck, cluck," said Cow.
"Bzzzzz, bzzzzz," said Bee.
"It is not you who has my moo,"
said Cow.

And on she went.

Cow passed Cat.
"Cluck, cluck," said Cow.
"Meow," said Cat.
"It is not you
who has my moo,"
said Cow.

And on she went.

Cow cooled her feet
in the creek.
"Cluck, cluck,"
said Cow.
"Glub, glub,"
said Fish.
"It is not you
who has my moo,"
said Cow.

And on she went.

Cow spotted Duck.

"Cluck, cluck," said Cow.

"Quack, quack," said Duck.

"It is not you who has my moo," said Cow.

And on she went.

Cow crossed the meadow.
"**Cluck, cluck,**" said Cow.
"**Maa, Maa,**" said Goat.
"It is not you who has my moo," said Cow.

And on she went.

Mouse darted past Cow.
"Cluck, cluck," said Cow.
"Squeak, squeak," said Mouse.
"It is not you who has my moo," said Cow.

And on she went.

Cow stepped 'round Snake.
"**Cluck, cluck,**" said Cow.
"**Sssss, sssss,**" said Snake.
"It is not you who has my moo," said Cow.

And on she went.

Cow rested under a tree.
"Cluck, cluck," said Cow.
"Chee, chee," said Squirrel.
"It is not you who has my moo," said Cow.

And on she went.

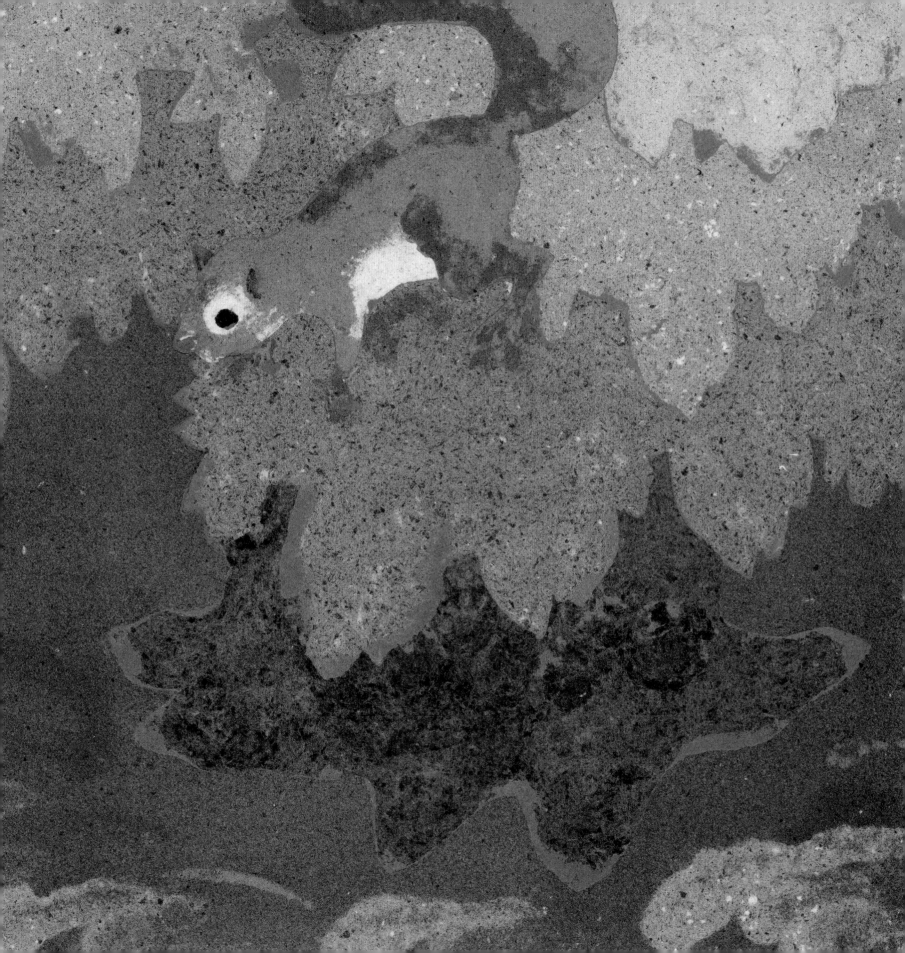

Cow spied Owl.
"Cluck, cluck," said Cow.

"**Who, who,**" said Owl.

"It is not you who has my moo,"
sighed Cow.

And she headed for the barn.

Cow shuffled past Hen.
"Cluck, cluck," said Cow.
"Moo, moo," said Hen.

"Hen!" cried Cow.
"It is YOU who has my MOO!"

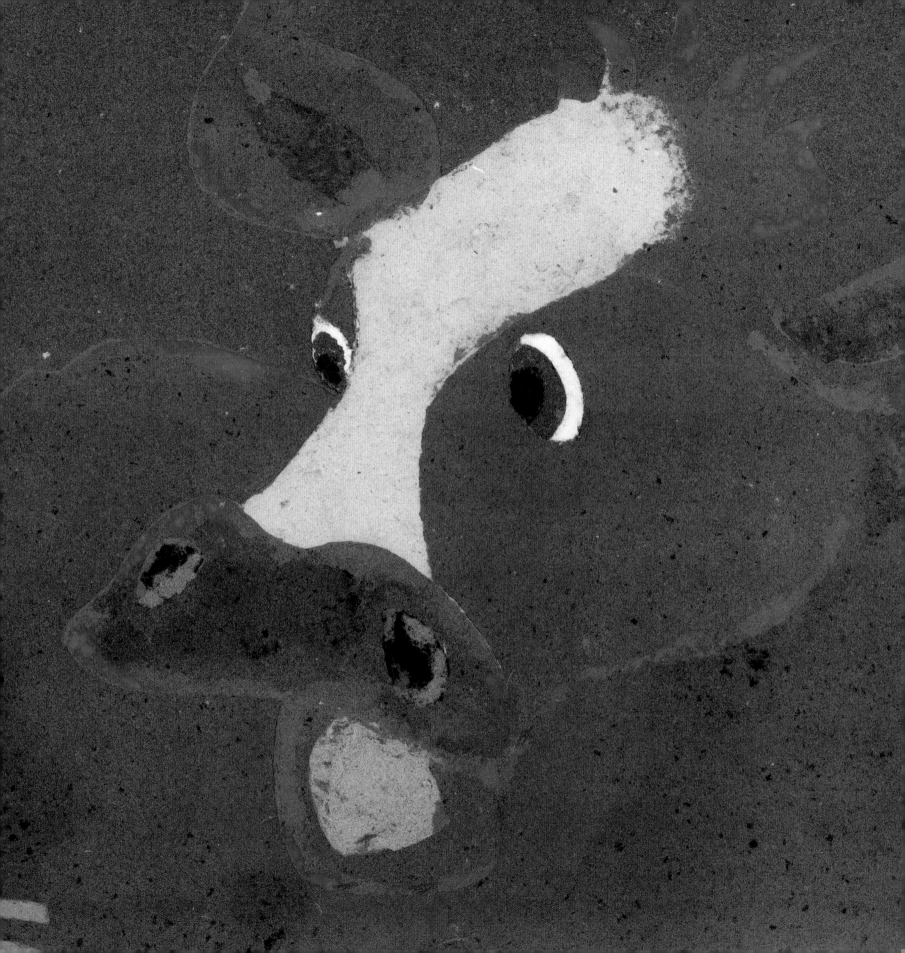

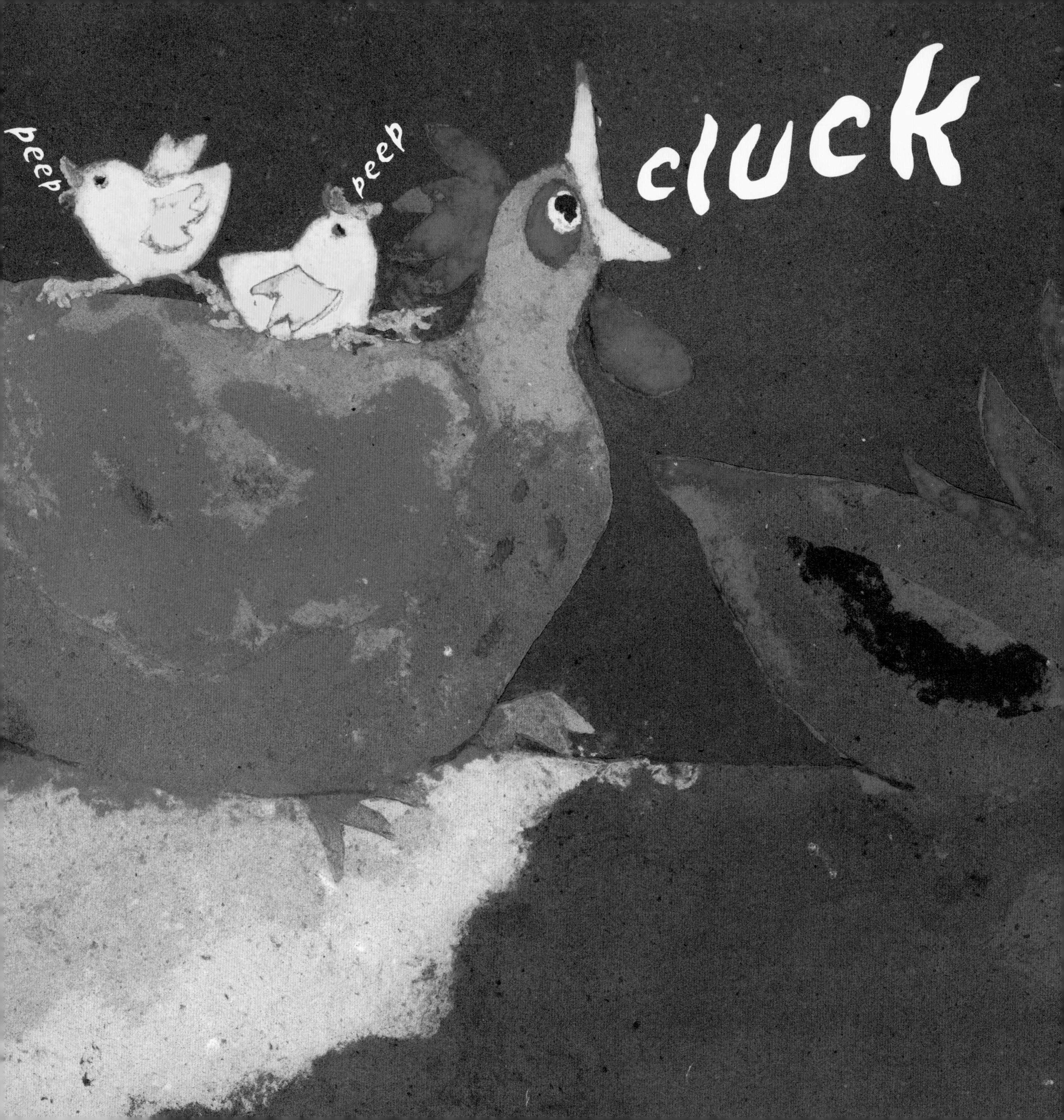
peep
peep
cluck

peep

moO